Original Korean text by Soon-jae Shin
Illustrations by Seung-min Oh

This English edition published by big & SMALL in 2016
by arrangement with Yeowon Media
English text edited by Joy Cowley

Distributed in the United States and Canada by
Lerner Publishing Group, Inc.
241 First Avenue North
Minneapolis, MN 55401 U.S.A.
www.lernerbooks.com

ISBN: 978-1-925248-60-9

Printed in Korea

The Bathtub

Written by Soon-jae Shin
Illustrated by Seung-min Oh
Edited by Joy Cowley

When Wilbur was little,
he had a bath every day
in his blue tub.

Wilbur loved his blue tub.
He kicked and splashed.

When he grew bigger,
he washed himself
and he washed his toys.

Sometimes, he had a bath
with his brother.

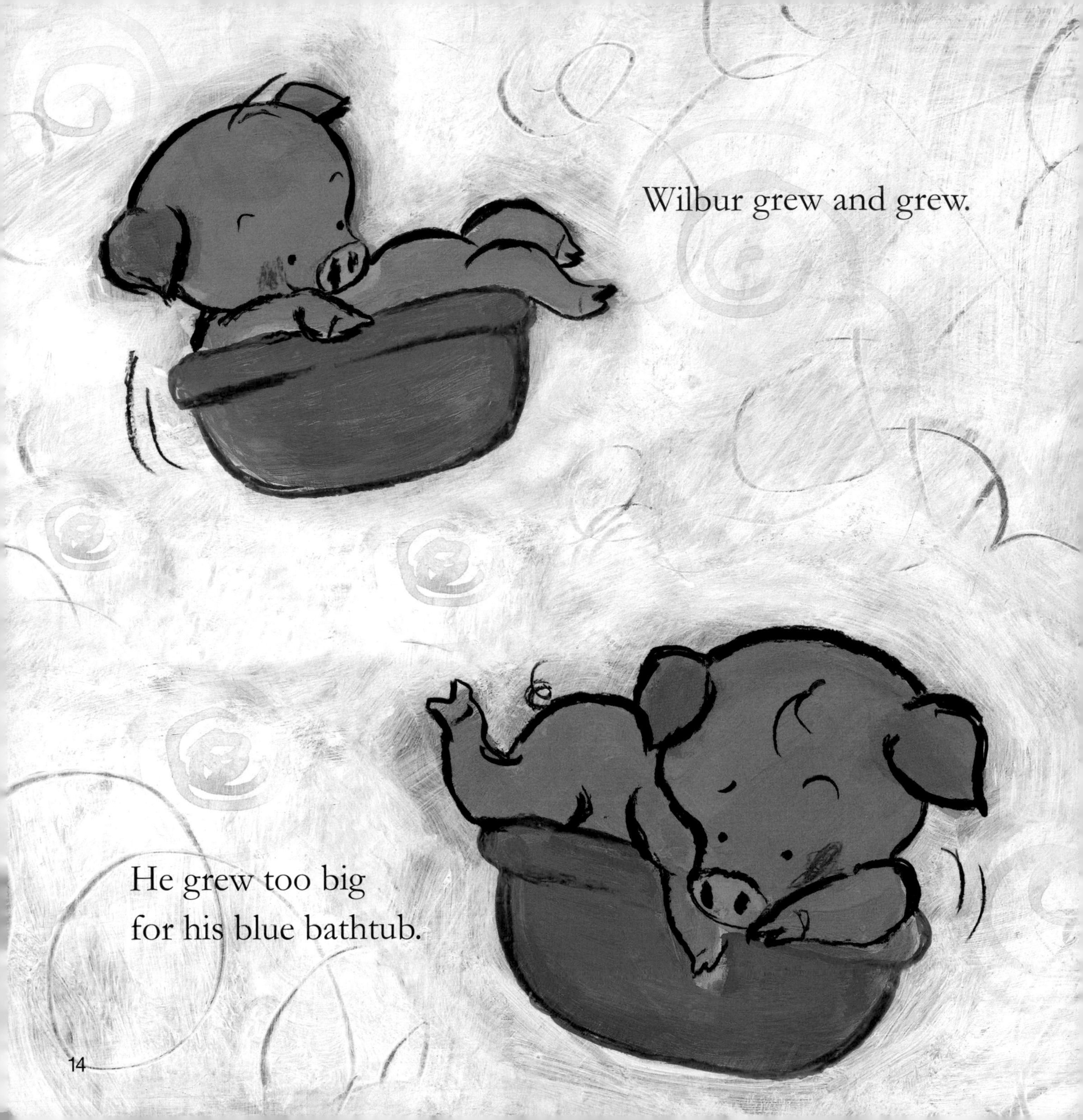

Wilbur grew and grew.

He grew too big
for his blue bathtub.

He fell out with a thud!

"Help!"
cried Wilbur.

Mother said, "Wilbur,
you need this new pink tub.
The blue tub is too small."

"I want my blue tub!"
cried Wilbur.

Father said, “Wilbur,
that old blue tub has to go.”

“No, no, no!” cried Wilbur.
“It is my blue bathtub!”

Wilbur went to bed
with his old blue bathtub.
He fell fast asleep.

When he woke up,
his blue bathtub had gone!

Wilbur ran outside.
"You can't throw out
my blue bathtub!
It's mine! It's mine!"

Father said, "Wilbur,
look at your new sled!
Do you want a ride?"

All that day, Wilbur had fun
in his blue bathtub sled.
Up the hill! Down the hill!
Up the hill! Down the hill!

Yahoo!

That night, Wilbur had a bath
in his new pink bathtub.
Tomorrow he would ride
in his blue sled again.